P9-CDO-891

KITTY PRYDE IS RUNNING AROUND A MANHATTAN MUSEUM WITH A MYSTICAL MASK WANTED BY THE NINJA CLAN KNOWN AS THE HAND, WHILE WOLVERINE AND THE HERO DAREDEVIL DEAL WITH NINJAS OF HIS OWN. JUST A TYPICAL DAY IN

WOLVERINE™ FIRST CLASS

HAND IN HAND PART 2

PETER DAVID writer
RONAN CLIQUET artist
ULISES ARREOLA colorist
VC's JOE CARAMAGNA letterer/production
WILLIAMS & QUINTANA cover
CHRIS ELIOPOULOS variant cover
RALPH MACCHIO consulting
NATHAN COSBY editor
JOE QUESADA editor in chief
DAN BUCKLEY publisher
ALAN FINE exec. producer

D. Williams '08

MARVEL Spotlight

Visit us at www.abdopublishing.com

Reinforced library bound editions published in 2014 by Spotlight, a division of the ABDO Group, PO Box 398166, Minneapolis, MN 55439. Spotlight produces high-quality reinforced library bound editions for schools and libraries. Published by agreement with Marvel Characters, Inc.

Printed in the United States of America, North Mankato, Minnesota.
042013
092013
This book contains at least 10% recycled material.

Library of Congress Cataloging-in-Publication Data

David, Peter (Peter Allen)
[Graphic novels. Selections]
Hand in hand / story by Peter David ; art by Ronan Cliquet. -- Reinforced library bound edition.
volumes cm. -- (Wolverine, first class)
"Marvel."
Summary: "Kitty Pryde usually likes museums, but wouldn't you know it...the art gallery that Wolverine's taken her to is run by the evil Hand (they're Ninja types), which means that Daredevil & Elecktra can't be too far away from the action"--Provided by publisher.
ISBN 978-1-61479-176-8 (part 1) -- ISBN 978-1-61479-177-5 (part 2)
1. Graphic novels. [1. Graphic novels. 2. Superheroes--Fiction.] I. Cliquet, Ronan, illustrator. II. Title.
PZ7.7.D374Han 2013
741.5'352--dc23

2013005933

All Spotlight books are reinforced library bindings and manufactured in the United States of America.

WHO... WHO IS *THAT?*
ELEKTRA.
ONE OF THE MOST FORMIDABLE, DEADLIEST ASSASSINS TO WALK THE EARTH.

FMMP
LOOKING GOOD, 'LEKTRA.
NOT YOU. YOU'VE GAINED WEIGHT. THE CUSHY LIFE AT YOUR LITTLE SCHOOL ILL-SUITS YOU.
FINE, I TAKE IT BACK. YA LOOK LIKE GARBAGE.
NAH, YA DON'T.
NO, I DON'T.
YOU TWO...KNOW EACH OTHER? YOU ARE FRIENDS WITH...AN ASSASSIN?
ENEMY OF MY ENEMY IS MY FRIEND. AND 'LEKTRA'S GOT NO LOVE FER THE HAND.
SHE KNOWS OF THEM?
I USED TO BE ONE OF THEM.
WHY DO THEY WANT SAGA-SAN DEAD? WHO HIRED THEM?
THEY DON'T CARE ABOUT HER. THEY CAME TO ATTACK YOU. TO MAKE SURE YOU DIDN'T INTERFERE.
WITH WHAT?

"THE MASK, WOLVERINE. THEY WANT THE MASK."
WH-WHA--?
"WHY DO THEY WANT THE MASK?"

IT IS A VALUABLE ART PIECE, BUT--
ITS COMMERCIAL VALUE IS IRRELEVANT. YOU HAVE NO IDEA WHAT THAT MASK IS.
BUT YOUR HUSBAND KNEW.
THAT'S WHY HE KEPT IT LOCKED AWAY IN AN IMPENETRABLE SAFE.

PUTTING IT ON DISPLAY WAS A HUGE MISTAKE.
IT IS A DEMON IN MASK FORM.
BUT I DON'T UNDERSTAND. IT'S JUST A DEMON MASK...
NO.

A DEMON THAT THE HAND WORSHIPS.
IF IT IS PLACED ON A WILLING SUBJECT UNDER A FULL MOON'S LIGHT, THE DEMON WILL MANIFEST.
SHING
AND IF THAT HAPPENS?
IT DOES NOT GO WELL FOR ALL CONCERNED.
THEN LET'S MAKE SURE THAT DON'T HAPPEN.

A FEW FLOORS DOWN...
YOUR MENTOR HAS SCHOOLED YOU WELL, DAREDEVIL.
TAUGHT ME EVERYTHING I KNOW.
INDEED.
BUT NOT EVERYTHING *I* KNOW.
NICELY DONE.
I WOULD HAVE CUT YOU OFF AT THE KNEES WERE YOU ANY SLOWER.
TRAGICALLY, AS FAST AS YOU ARE...

...YOU ARE NOT FAST *ENOUGH*.
SEEKING TO RETURN THE FAVOR OF MY PUMMELING YOU?
UNFORTUNATE. ONCE AGAIN--
--YOU ARE *NOT* WORTH WASTING ANY MORE TIME UP--
--OOOOOOOONNNNN!!!

SORRY I HAVEN'T GIVEN YOU ENOUGH OF A CHALLENGE.
THEN AGAIN, IF YOU'D PAID ATTENTION TO ME TYING MY BILLY CLUB WIRE AROUND YOUR ANKLE INSTEAD OF TALKING ABOUT HOW *FABULOUS* YOU ARE--
--WE COULD BOTH HAVE SAVED OURSELVES SOME TIME.
KRAAAAASH

THIS THE SAFE ROOM, SAGA-SAN?
YES, LOGAN-SAN.
SMELLS CLEAN. NO NINJAS HIDING INSIDE.
SMELLS--?
TRUST ME. NOW GET IN AND STAY THERE UNTIL I SAY IT'S SAFE TO COME OUT.
BUT WHAT ABOUT THE NINJAS? WHAT ARE YOU GOING TO DO?
THOOM
WHAT I DO BEST.

THIS IS INSANE. I'VE GOT TO FIND LOGAN, GET OUT OF HERE BEFORE--
A HOCKEY PUCK? WHO'S PLAYING HOCKEY IN--?

OUTSIDE, SIX SECONDS AGO...
THIS IS RIDICULOUS. MY MOTHER'S GONNA KILL ME.
"SARAH, I DON'T LIKE YOU HANGING OUT WITH THAT KITTY PRYDE. THERE'S SOMETHING ABOUT HER THAT JUST BOTHERS ME."
MAN, WHEN I GET HOME, SHE'S GONNA BLOW UP--
KRHOOOM
HUH--?!?!
HOLY CRUD!!!!
TERRORISTS!!!

STUPID. STUPID STUPID STUPID.
⫩KOFF⫨ ⫩KOFF⫨
I LET MYSELF GET CAUGHT TOTALLY FLATFOOTED. IF I HADN'T PHASED AT THE LAST MICROSECOND, I'D BE UNCONSCIOUS OR WORSE.
THE MASK. WHERE'S THE--?
KITTY--!
KARLSH
ARE YOU OKAY?! WHAT WERE YOU DOING WITH THIS?
WHAT WAS THAT EXPLOSION?
IT'S COMPLICATED!
SO I'M SUPPOSED TO-- WHAT? WAIT FOR THE CLIFF'S NOTES VERSION?
AND WHO'S THAT?!? KITTY, WHAT'S GOING ON?!?
I DUNNO! IT'S NOT LIKE HE CAME WITH ME!

NOW WE END THIS!
IN THAT, YOU ARE CORRECT!
WHAT'S HAPPENING?!? I DON'T UNDERSTAND--
UNDERSTANDING CAN BE YOURS, MY CHILD...
WHA--?
PLACE ME ON YOUR FACE... AND ALL WILL BE MADE CLEAR. I SWEAR TO YOU.
AND YOU'LL NEED FEAR NOTHING-- NOT STRANGE BEINGS, NOT EVEN YOUR MOTHER'S SCOLDINGS-- EVER AGAIN.

NO! KID! DROP THAT MASK--
IT IS NOT MEANT FOR ONE SUCH AS SHE! PUT IT--!
TOO LATE! AAAAHHAHAHAHA! TOO LATE!
I WILL LIVE! BREATHE! FEEL THE COOL AIR UPON MY BODY! FEEL MY HEART PUMPING BLOOD IN THE HEAT OF COMBAT! NOW--

--LET THE WRATH OF SHINIGAMI BE FELT!

WHAT DO WE DO?!?
I VOTE WE DO UNTO IT BEFORE IT DOES UNTO US.
BUT... BUT SARAH'S IN THERE! THAT THING'S POSSESSING HER!
BAD LUCK FOR HER.
NO.
YOU DON'T GET T'SAY NO T'ME, KID.
I'M NOT A KID. I'M THIRTEEN AND A HALF.
I DON'T CARE IF YA HIT THE BIG THIRTEEN POINT SEVEN FIVE. THAT AIN'T YER FRIEND NO MORE.
OH, NOBLE SHINIGAMI! I AM AKUMA, LORD HIGH OF--
I KNOW WHO YOU ARE. YOU WISHED TO UNLEASH ME...
...NOT IN THE NAME OF MY GLORY, BUT TO USURP MY POWER FOR YOUR OWN ENDS.
WHAT FOOLS THESE MORTALS BE.
FA-QUNG

NOW THEN...
...WHO ENDS NEXT?

DESTROY THE MASK! IT'S THE ONLY CHANCE!

THEN YOU HAVE NO CHANCE.

NO MERE METAL WEAPON CAN DESTROY IT. NOR CAN IT BE REMOVED BY ANY MEANS SAVE FROM THE INSIDE OUT...
...NAMELY PEELING THE SKULL AFTER DECAPITATION, AND IF YOU BELIEVE I WILL LET YOU GET THAT CLOSE--
THINK AGAIN!

EH?
A LITTLE HELP--?
WE'RE ON IT!
OOOOOOF! YOU...DARE!
PHUP
WELL, WHEN THEY CALL YOU "DAREDEVIL" YOU KIND OF HAVE TO LIVE UP TO THE NAME.

"LIVING UP" TO ANYTHING WILL NO LONGER BE A CONCERN FOR YOU. FOR ANY OF YOU.
HAVE TO TIME THIS PERFECTLY. IF I DON'T...SARAH'S DONE FOR.
PHASE MY FIST THROUGH, HARDEN IT JUST ENOUGH TO KNOCK THE MASK FREE...
WHA--?
HOW DARE YOU!!!!
Y'THINK THAT'S BAD? HERE'S WORSE NEWS:

MY CLAWS MAY BE METAL WEAPONS--
ZZNNG
--BUT THEY AIN'T NO "MERE."
NOOOOOOO!!!!

K-KITTY?
YOU OKAY, SARAH? A GAS MAIN EXPLODED AND YOU PASSED OUT FROM THE EXCITEMENT.
PASSED OUT--?
YUP.

I COULD SWEAR THERE WERE SOME... SOME PEOPLE IN COSTUMES...
NOPE. NOBODY LIKE THAT HERE.
YOU POSITIVE?
ABSO-TOOTLY.
CAN... CAN WE GO HOME NOW?
SURE.

THAT WAS GUTSY, THE WAY YA STOOD UP TO ME BEFORE.
THANKS.
DON'T MAKE A HABIT OF IT.
YESSIR.

YOU THINK SHE'S GOING TO ***REMEMBER*** ANY OF IT?
NOT IF WE'RE LUCKY. THEN AGAIN, THERE'S NO PREDICTING MEMORY.
FER INSTANCE, I KEEP THINKIN' THERE'S SOMETHING I'M FORGETTING. SOMETHING IMPORTANT.

"AH WELL. IT'LL PROBABLY COME T'ME."
PANG
PANG
PANG
LOGAN? ELEKTRA? IS IT ***SAFE*** TO COME OUT YET?
HELLO?

HELLO?
EN